W9-CBD-158

CONTENTS

Diary of a Roblox Noob: High School

by

Robloxia Kid

Two Sovereigns Publishing

ENTRY 1: THE FIRST DAY AND THE BIG GANG

After doing things one way for a long time, everybody wants a change. Sooner or later, you want to change the pace, or throw a little variety in the mix, so to speak. It's just the way everybody is. As one of my former friends remarked: 'Variety is the spice of life.'

That's exactly how I felt when I entered Roblox High School. I'm Noob, and I've had more than my fair share of Roblox games where I got blown to bits, or got smashed up pretty good. I blew up a lotta other guys in my time too. And I am not saying I didn't like it. On the contrary, the constant stream of adventures excited me! But after the events of the Murder Mystery, where the stakes were so high, I felt that I needed a break from all that. I even began to wonder if there is more to life. After all, plenty of Roblox players take joy in the routine of playing one game over and over again. And so I hoped to find that calm in life when I agreed to accompany Joe to Roblox High School – a peaceful and uneventful server where everyone is happy. Or so I thought.

Yup, it was back to school for this Noob. I know what you're thinking. Most people cannot wait to graduate from school, while I strive to get there. I know it's odd, but whilst school is hell for some, others have the best time of their lives! And so I kept that in mind while hoping to discover what kind of person I am. Plus, I did need a change of pace from all the crazy action stuff in the other games, so this was probably the best place to start fresh. I was sure this would be anything but boring.

Being new anywhere is always intimidating. But I guess, as a Noob, that's my fate! There's just no going around that. On my first day, I walked around the halls and heard everyone talking and chattering with each other. It was really scary because it seemed like everyone knew everyone else. I felt like I was the only one not talking to anyone in the hallway. How would I possibly be able to make a friend here?

So I decided not to focus on making friends, at least not for the moment. What else do students do in school? That's right! I resolved to actually study. Perhaps the friends would follow in time. Or if not, Joe was supposed to arrive soon, and I would be fine either way. But I was still pleasantly surprised to learn that I would not have to wait as long as I thought.

I took an empty seat in the classroom. It was full of students of different shapes and sizes.

"Hey. You're new in class, aren't you?"

The kid with the big glasses that sat beside me asked my name. Honestly, he looked pretty clever with those big glasses and I didn't think he would be the sociable type. Shame on me for thinking that.

"Yeah. How about you?" I asked.

"I've been in high school for as long as I can remember. I've been playing pretty long and I think I've managed to make a name for myself in the school. I'm Levi by the way."

"Cool name, Levi. I'm Noob."

"Nice to meet you Noob."

Levi was interrupted by a huge pie that flew in his face. It was nothing harmful like the other shots I endured in past games. His body didn't fly off into several pieces, no. But it still must have been very embarrassing!

"Pie fight!"

The other kid who threw the pie at Levi was a big guy with a mohawk moustache and a goatee. He had a pretty cool custom look that screamed 'bully' all over him. It wasn't hard to see that I would really not get along with this guy.

Instead of doing anything Levi just sat there and took even more pies to the face. The big kid's gang started throwing the stuff all over and the class reacted with wild laughter. A few of the pies began to hit me too.

"Hey! Cut it out!" I said.

"Yeah, what are you going to do about it Newbie?"

This big bully was really beginning to get

on my nerves. Who did he think he was? I couldn't just take such abuse on my first day!

I stood up and approached the big guy. I didn't know what or how I was going to stand up to him, but I wasn't going to take that kind of abuse lying down.

"Hey! Get back in your chair, Noob! That's Big Man Stipples! No one messes with him and the Big Gang!"

Levi was literally shaking in his boots as I approached Stip Stip. The other members of the Big Gang were just laughing at me, and daring me to try something. I should probably have been afraid too, just like Levi. After all, I was outnumbered four-to-one, and this 'Big Gang' was clearly the dominant group in school. Still, I was so angry at Stipples for throwing pies our way. Besides, Momma Noob didn't raise a coward. No way!

"You really want to make something of

this, don't you?"

Big Man Stipples was really mad now. I expected him to charge right at me, but I didn't care! I was mad too! I was almost roaring and ready to prove to everyone that I was no chicken, and he was no 'Big Man' like he said he was. The whole class was suddenly silent and it was clear that they were all expecting a big fight too. School fight!

What happened next just blew my mind! I expected Stipples to charge at me or something. No way! It didn't happen like that at all. No way at all! Suddenly, someone stood between us, someone much smaller than me or Stipples. This guy had a crew cut and shades and had a really bad attitude. It seemed like he was as crazy as he was small.

"You want to mess with Big Man Stipples, you're going to have to get through me first! Me, Scrappy Randy!"

I didn't know whether to get mad or laugh! I couldn't believe the nerve of this guy. Scrappy Randy was bad enough, but Stipples was really a jerk! What kind of a 'Big Man' had someone else fight his battles for him?

The whole class waited as I stared Scrappy Randy down. Behind him, Big Man Stipples had disappeared behind some other kids, who were clearly the other members of the Big Gang. This was really going to be a big throwdown at high school!

"What's going on here?"

A guy with a cool-looking white lab coat entered. He had big white hair and reminded me of somebody smart.

"Nothing Professor Spooky Hair!"

Once they saw the Prof enter the room, everybody sat down. I would later learn that Professor Spooky Hair was the class moderator and Science and Chemistry teacher at Roblox High School. He had the look of intelligence and authority that most kids would respect. I guess they did get a good teacher to try to contain our rowdy class.

"Good. Now that that's done, let's get on with the lesson. Oh! I see we have a new student here in class!"

Professor Spooky Hair called me over to introduce myself to everyone. I thought I probably didn't even need to do that anymore after what had just happened. I approached the front of the class but before I could speak, Scrappy Randy whispered in my ear.

"This isn't over by a longshot, Noob!"

"Bring it on!" I whispered back.

Levi was still cowering in my seat but I wasn't about to back down. I thought I needed a change in pace, but it surely didn't mean that I wouldn't stand up against these bullies. Do they know who I am?! I've managed to break out of prison and save an entire sever of players back in Murder Mystery. I'm never going to back down from a bunch of bullies like the Big Gang. They're not going to see me crack, no way!

The whole day passed without any incident after that. I'm sure that I haven't seen the last of Scrappy Randy, Big Man Stipples, and those other kids in his crazy gang. Still, I'm also very positive that I'll meet some more friends aside from Levi as well. This is far from over.

ENTRY 2: THE SMOKE CLOUD AND A FAMILIAR FACE

"Okay, class. Today we're going to the chemistry lab to do some experiments."

My second day in class opened up with Professor Spooky Hair ordering the class to the Chemistry room for some basic experiments. I admit – chemistry was never really one of my stronger points, but I kept an open mind.

'Who knows? Maybe something interesting will come out of this.' I thought to myself.

I didn't know just how right I would be.

We all trooped down to the Chemistry Room. I walked with Levi and the Big Gang passed us by. I saw Big Man Stipples snarl at us, along with his attack dog, Scrappy Randy. I noticed the other kids walking beside them. There was a tall kid with large glasses, and another kid with a large mouth. Beside him was a girl with a Japanese-style, schoolgirl outfit.

"That's the other members of the Big Gang. The tall thin kid with glasses is Marvin Mangler and the kid with a long mouth is Paulson. His girlfriend is the Japanese-looking girl, Kitsy E. Katty. They're pretty much all of the Big Gang here at school."

I turned around and saw a fat kid walking beside me and Levi. The kid had a round belly and a reverse cap.

"I'm E.U. Gene and I are really glad that you stood up to those bullies! That took a lot of guts."

"Not so loud, E.U.! They're going to hear, and once they do, we're done for!"

"Will you stop being so afraid, Levi? I know they're big and tough, but we can't just let them have their way around here in school! Isn't that right, Noob?"

I had only been in Roblox High School for just two days but it appeared as if I was already in the thick of things. I guess wherever I go, I end up right in the middle of trouble.

"Uh, yeah. Yeah, of course it is!"

We all trooped into the Chemistry Room. Professor Spooky Hair gave a long rant about how to mix the chemicals and compounds. I wasn't even listening and could barely stay awake. The other kids were mixing the compounds already and seemed to understand what he was saying. I was really relieved that this was going to be a group activity. That way, I could lean on my more chemically inclined classmates. I was conveniently paired with E.U. and Levi. My two groupmates seemed to show a passion and a knack for Chemistry that I just didn't have. They breezed through the computations and the mixtures, almost as if they were actually ahead of the Prof's explanations. These guys were geniuses in their fields. The only thing was that they were also arguing.

"Boy, am I glad I've got you two to carry me on this activity! I just don't understand any of this." I said.

EU and Levi ignored me and continued bickering. I couldn't even understand what they were arguing about.

"The yellow liquid goes in there! Then we should pour the violet compound there to have the desired effect!"

"No! I don't think this is a good idea. The

resulting mixture could really be volatile!"

Volatile? I didn't understand what was going on, but it was clear that EU Gene was trying to tell Levi not to do something. Levi on the other hand, was mixing different compounds with a flurry now. He was juggling, and mixing and matching much similar to some kind of performer.

"Okay. What's going on here?" I asked them.

Levi turned towards me and grinned. He grinned in a different way that really creeped me out. This wasn't the timid kid I met on my first day. When I saw that smile, I knew something was up.

"You'll see. Everyone's going to see, especially the Big Gang!"

"No! Stop him Noob!"

EU's warning came too late. I was still trying to figure out what was going on here, so I couldn't act in time. Before I knew what was happening, Levi walked towards the Big Gang's corner where they were trying to do the experiment as Professor Spooky Hair had directed.

"What are you doing here? Finally got gutsy enough to take a stand?"

It was Big Man Stipples. He was laughing at Levi as he walked right up to him. He wouldn't be laughing in a very short while.

That was when it happened. Levi tossed a vial of strange mixed compounds right at Stipples and the other members of the Big Gang. The vial exploded in a loud 'BOOM' sound that was heard all over the Chemistry Room.

"What's going on?" Professor Spooky Hair said.

He was shocked but it was too late. Levi had tossed the strange mixture of compounds that he and EU had been mixing earlier. The vial exploded and covered the entire room in a thick cloud of smoke.

"What happened?" I asked, being shocked myself.

Everyone was stumbling around the room. We all couldn't see anything.

"This is what I was afraid of! Levi tossed that compound of mixed chemicals right at the Big Gang! It's highly unstable and I don't know what it could do!"

I didn't like the tone of fear in EU Gene's voice. He sounded really terrified. Whatever those chemicals were, they sure seemed like bad stuff. At least that was judging from EU's reaction.

When the smoke cleared everyone was still standing in place. There didn't seem to be any damage, and it looked like everything was just one big bag of hot air that literally exploded.

"What just happened?"

It was Professor Spooky. He sure sounded really angry and confused and for good reason. When Spooky Hair shouted, everyone went quiet and all eyes turned on him. After the short moment of silence, everyone started laughing hysterically. I have to admit – I was also laughing now. I couldn't help myself. Everyone was laughing at Professor Spooky Hair.

"What's so funny? Tell me! Keep quiet everyone!"

Spooky was losing it. He just didn't know what was going on. He turned towards a nearby mirror and got the shock of his life. His once white hair that once exploded everywhere was now gone. In it's place was a giant button on top of his head. Professor Spooky Hair now had no hair!!!

Once he realized what had happened, he turned towards Levi with anger.

"What have you done?" he said.

"What have you done?"

It was Big Man Stipples. He was now turning towards Levi with anger as well. Paulson, Marvin the Mangler, Kitsy E. Katty, and Scrappy Randy were all enraged at Levi now. The laughter was non-stop. Everyone had been laughing at Professor Spooky, but now everyone was also laughing at the entire Big Gang as well, and for good reason. They all looked completely different from their previous selves. Their heads had all been turned into balloons with smileys. Somehow Levi's potion had mixed up the chemical makeup of the Big Gang and Professor Spooky Hair. Their custom appearances had all been messed up.

"We'll get you for this!"

Scrappy Randy was so angry now, and turned to try to punch Levi. It was hopeless. He slipped and fell along with the entire Big Gang. Apparently, once the mixture exploded it also left a liquid residue on the floor where they all stood. The whole Big Gang fell flat on the floor making things much worse for them than it already was.

Everyone was cracking with laughter now. It was the most humiliating moment for the schoolyard bullies. Professor Spooky Hair left the room in a huff. The entire Big Gang were lying on the floor. They had been reduced to emoticon balloons, literally. Now, even Levi was laughing. We all knew he would get serious detention time for this, but no one really cared. The moment was just too silly and great to think of anything else.

"Everyone! Get back to your seats and keep quiet!"

We all turned at the new voice that entered the Chemistry Room. I also turned with a start. I couldn't believe my ears. I recognized that voice.

"I'm the substitute teacher now for this crazy class, and I am restoring order right now!"

I turned to the new teacher. I recognized those Roblox features anywhere.

"Joe?"

I asked the question more out of surprise than inquiry. Of course, I recognized Joe instantly.

"Hi Noob!"

We stood and just stared at each other for a long moment. The school day's already long over, and I still can't believe that Joe will be my teacher in class. All of a sudden Roblox High School really got super interesting. I can't wait for tomorrow to start.

ENTRY 3: THE EMOJI GANG

We started the new school day minus Levi. That was to be expected. It was no surprise that he got serious detention time for pulling off that hilarious stunt in the Chemistry Lab. But I also noticed that there were fewer students in class today. Meanwhile, the Big Gang were still wearing their balloon heads and looking very sour and angry. There was nothing that they could do. Their terrible customization looked permanent.

"Okay. Professor Spooky Hair is

indisposed and will not be able to teach the class for the foreseeable future. He's too busy trying to make an antidote for that strange potion that Levi zapped him with. So you guys over there at the back can rest easy. He's working right now to try to reverse the effects."

Everyone laughed as Joe finished his short speech. Everyone but the Big Gang. They were all in a very sour mood. I actually couldn't blame them.

"I'll be handling your class in the meantime, until Professor Spooky can get back to work."

There was a short hush as everyone waited for Joe to continue speaking.

"Until then, well. Uhm,"

Joe paused with his words. He was struggling for what to say.

"Oh, what the hell! Free period for everyone!"

There was a loud cheer that rang out from the entire class. Everybody began chatting away and socializing. I wasn't really surprised that Joe would declare a free period. I never really saw him as the academic type anyway. With Joe as the teacher, I was sure that the class would have a lot of these periods a lot more often.

While everyone was chatting away, I decided to get straight to the matter and talk to Joe.

"Joe!"

"Noob! Sorry it took me so long to come."

"It's alright Joe. What happened thought? Why are you a teacher?"

"Well, I always wanted to be a high school teacher. I am sorry I forgot to mention it before you let Murder Mystery" Joe said.

"Somehow, you don't strike me as the teacher-type." I said.

"Heh. I guess I can't really blame you for thinking that, Noob. I just called a free period on my first class with you guys. Maybe I ought to be more teacher-like."

I shook my head.

"Nah. Don't do anything that'll crimp your style. Besides, this is a lot more fun than studying!"

"Speaking of fun, you arrived here right in time."

"Really? Why is that?"

"Well, the school prom is coming just around the corner."

"Oh that's right! Well you have you picked your date yet?"

Joe's announcement surprised me a lot. I didn't even think of getting a date. Sure, having a date at prom night would be awesome. I was never really the romantic type, but with prom night coming, I had to get a date! I guess I would have to ask some girl out for the upcoming prom. I just didn't know how I would go about it. I was still a new guy in school. This would be a little tougher than I thought.

"I better find a date then." I said.

"You want a date for the prom? Let me give you a little advice. If you want to get a date, it's best to be a lot more active in school. Maybe you should go join the prom committee."

"Really? You think so?"

"I know so. Get into the swing of things a lot more. Before you know it, you'll know most of the school's students and then you'll find a great date for the prom."

"I hope you're right, Joe. Maybe I will follow that advice of yours. It's worth a shot. So just how do you get into the prom committee?"

"Well, first you have to find a goat and sacrifice it in the forbidden forest. Once you do that, there is another ritual you have to perform. It takes about a year to complete, but"

"It's not funny Joe! I need a date soon so tell me, how do I join the committee?" – I cut him off.

"Relax Noob! I am just messing with you. It's real easy! Just go to their office down the hall. You've got some free time anyway, so why not go there now?"

It was a great suggestion! Going to the prom committee and asking around would sure be a lot better than goofing around in the classroom. I decided to do just what Joe said and go there immediately.

Before I left, I spotted the Big Gang in the corner of my eye, and it didn't look good. They were arguing among themselves but I couldn't understand what they were saying. The whole class was just too noisy because of Joe's free period. Big Man Stipples pointed towards me and Joe. If I didn't know better, I thought they were arguing because I was talking with Joe.

Joe noticed it too.

"Is there a problem, Mr. Big Man?"

"Nothing. Nothing at all."

Big Man Stipples then proceeded to walk out of the classroom. He and the entire Big Gang looked pretty ridiculous with their balloon heads expressing angry emoticons. Perhaps they should have been called the Emojis now.

"What's with him?" I asked.

"I don't know, but something tells me that while I'm your teacher, I'm really going to have my hands full containing that crazy group of theirs. I don't agree with what Levi did but I don't blame him either." Joe said.

"I don't envy you, man."

"Never mind. Run along now and get to

that prom committee!"

"Thanks!"

That was Joe for you. He was always a great guy, even back when we were doing hard time. He was the kind of guy you could easily befriend. I just didn't know if he could really control the Big Gang. But I guess he could, since he managed to fool Frank. And that guy was not easy to overcome. Plus, now that the gang were the Emojis, they seemed pretty ridiculous.

I went to the prom committee office and promptly entered. Get it? I entered the prom committee *promptly*. At least I am not a Noob in jokes and humor. Anyway, there was a girl sitting at the front desk. She had blonde hair tied up in a ponytail with an eager smile for anyone.

"Hi. I'm Noob, and I want to join the prom committee."

"Great! You're in!"

"What? That's it?"

I was shocked at how eagerly the girl just let me join the committee. Thank god there was no goat sacrifice after all.

"Yeah. That's it. I'm really glad someone actually joined me."

"Wait. You said 'me?' Not 'us?' "

"Oh yeah. The prom committee is now up to two members! You and me!"

I couldn't believe this! How could a committee even be a committee with just one member, and now just two members? We didn't even know each other yet! This was beyond silly!

"I don't understand! Why were there no members before me?"

The girl took a deep breath and sighed.

"It's pretty sad, I know. Let's face it. People would rather attend a party instead of organizing it. Also, I've noticed that some students have stopped coming to class recently. I thought I would have to be the only one to organize prom, but now that you came along I'm saved!

"Wow!"

"Pardon me. I'm Patty. And you are…?"

"Noob."

"Nice to meet you Noob!"

"Likewise!"

Patty looked like a really friendly kind of girl and I was sure that I would get along with her. Still, the task of organizing a whole prom with only her looked more than a little daunting.

"Well, now that you're here you might as well get started! I need you to cut some decorations over there and.."

"Whoa! Whoa! Time for work already?"

Patty frowned at me.

"We're the only two members of the prom committee! We can't just sit around and wait for anyone else to do our jobs! The prom is just a few days away!"

Unfortunately, Patty was right. How could I even think of just sitting around? The rest of my day was spent helping Patty cut decorations, arrange invites, and other tedious organizing activities. I was so drained and exhausted when it was all done!

"There. We've managed to do some work, but not nearly enough. Come back tomorrow for more work. Just tell your moderator about it. He'll excuse you from class immediately. And don't worry about today either. You'll be excused as well. After all, this is a special school activity."

"Thanks Patty." I said. Wow, I could just skip classes organizing the party? This was some great tip from Joe. I guess now we are even, considering that I was almost stuck in Murder Mystery for the rest of my days because he asked me to help.

"Don't mention it!"

I ran back to class eager to talk to Joe again. The bell had rung and it was time to go home. Still, I decided to talk with my friend for awhile just to catch up.

"Joe! I'm on the prom committee and I'll be taking a day off tomorrow from class to finish some prom arrangements."

When I entered the classroom, Joe heard me but did not respond. He just nodded silently, looking really serious. This wasn't the usual active Joe that I knew.

"What's wrong?" I asked.

"It's Big Man Stipples. He didn't show up for class the entire day. I'm a little concerned." Joe said.

"I wouldn't be. If I know him, he probably just cut class for the entire day. The whole Emoji gang looked real mad that we're friends and all."

"Emoji gang?"

I smiled.

"That's what I decided to call them now that they've got those balloon heads."

Joe smiled and his serious mood seemed to lift for awhile.

"Cute. I think it might actually catch on. Maybe you're right Noob. Still, I'm very concerned. I've got a bad feeling about this."

"I don't. Just wait. He'll turn up tomorrow."

I still don't have a bad feeling about it. Joe tends to worry too much. Doing hard time can do that to someone. I'm a lot more concerned with organizing the prom with Patty. That's a lot more pressing for me now. I am taking a break from adventures, aren't I?

ENTRY 4: DODGEBALL!

The preparations for the prom were in full swing now. I spent two whole schooldays preparing stuff with Patty. I was in charge of just about everything, and she was swamped with a lot of work too. After all, we were the only members of this so-called 'prom committee' and no one was joining us. What a joke! Patty was so right about no one wanting to buckle down to the hard work in this place. So right indeed.

Well, I had to go to school today. I had already missed two whole days preparing with Patty. If I missed another I would really miss out on a lot of schoolwork, excused or not. Worse than that? I still couldn't find a date for the prom! After all, my plan with the prom committee didn't really go as I'd imagined. What a bummer!

I reported back to class right on schedule for our Gym class. Well, this had to be a fun class. After all, this was Roblox! What else did you do but bounce around here? This was going to be a great breeze!

"Hey man! It's been awhile!"

"Yeah, we were starting to miss you!"

It was EU and Levi who greeted me once I got back. Sure they seemed to be the nerds of the class, but so what? They were fun to be with and easy to get along. That was enough for me.

"Hi EU! Speak for yourself Levi! You got detention for that stunt you pulled off a few days back!"

Levi smiled at me. This kid was really proving to be a lot more than the scared geek that I first met on the first day of school.

"Hey. Don't tell me you didn't get a big kick out of it." Levi said.

There was more than a little glee and satisfaction written on his face when he spoke.

"Okay. Okay. I admit it. It was really fun seeing those guys get what they deserved back there."

"It's really funny 'cause everybody calls them the Emoji gang now! No one's afraid of them anymore!" EU said.

The Emoji gang. Well what do you know? Joe was right. It actually did catch on faster than I expected.

I decided to keep to myself the fact that I coined their new name. I was more than satisfied that they got humiliated like that.

After all, no one likes a bully.

"It would really be funny if only something strange wasn't happening." EU said. His face suddenly turned serious.

"Really? What's that?"

"Haven't you heard? Big Man Stipples is still missing! He didn't return from cutting class when you joined the prom committee."

"Whoa."

I was almost knocked for a loop with that bit of information. It had been two days since I was absent on excused leave. What had happened to Stipples?

"You ask me, he got what was coming to him. Who cares if he disappeared anyway?" Levi said.

I could detect the anger and vindication in Levi's voice. I couldn't blame him, but someone else heard him and definitely blamed him.

"That's not all, guys." – EU started. "There are strange rumors going around the school. I've heard that he might not be the only one gone. In fact, I even…"

Suddenly EU was interrupted.

"You think this is funny? You think that I don't know that you had something to do with the Big Man's disappearance? You'll pay for all of this trouble you're causing!"

It was Scrappy Randy. He approached Levi angrily with a mad emoticon face on his balloon head.

"Go pick on a pin or something!" I said.

"You and your friends are gonna get what's coming to you Noob!"

"Hey, break it off!"

The voice of our muscular Gym teacher stopped us from duking it out right then and there.

"There'll be no fights in my class. You just

take it out in Dodgeball!"

The Gym teacher handed us some rubber balls and we all began throwing the balls like crazy. He said that he didn't want any fights to break out, but he sure had a strange way of enforcing the rules.

There was a long session of ball-tossing. I admit it was pretty satisfying seeing Scrappy Randy get hit by rubber balls several times. This went on for the entire period and it was a lot of fun while it lasted.

The whole school day passed with no incident. Professor Spooky was still out of it along with his hair and Joe was still our head moderator. I had a feeling he would be our moderator indefinitely. He treated us with another series of free periods that left us doing nothing but chatting among ourselves. Well, I didn't mind, and so did the rest of the class. Who doesn't want free time anyway?

ENTRY 5: THE MYSTERY CONTINUES

Okay, now this is getting freaky really fast. This is no laughing matter anymore. It's been more than a week since I've been going to Roblox High School, and now things are really getting weird! There have been more disappearances lately. Now, the whole Emoji gang has just vanished! This is really getting weird. People really didn't notice when Big Man Stipples vanished but now his whole gang vanished. That's really gotten people talking.

"Who cares if they're all missing? I don't

see what's the big fuss!"

Levi was really happy that they were all gone. I have to admit that I was also pretty upbeat about it. There were no more bullies in class and that had to be a good thing. Still, disappearing students is never a good thing either, so we had to get to the bottom of this regardless of what we felt.

"Hey man. Disappearing students are serious stuff." EU said.

"Yeah but these kids were nothing but bullies and douchebags. Good riddance!"

Levi was really beginning to sound suspicious with all his rants. He did manage to mess them up big time with his chemical bomb. Was it that much of a stretch to think that he was responsible for their vanishing?

Joe declared another free period for us. This was getting to be a habit for him.

"Noob, come here." he said.

"Yeah? What's up Joe?"

"You know what's up. The Emoji gang disappearing has got the whole school wondering what's going on! Because I had to have the bad luck of accepting this substitute teaching gig from Professor Spooky Hair, I'm getting a bad rep for it! I am your Head Moderator, after all! We have to get to the bottom of this."

I could really see that Joe was worried and for good reason. I wouldn't want to be in his shoes now. I also never thought about how strange and funny it was that the school hired an ex inmate to teach. Maybe they didn't' know? Still, he was my friend, and I had to try to help him.

"Don't worry, Joe. I'll ask around. Maybe I can get to the bottom of all of this." I said.

"Thanks Noob. I knew I could count on you."

Joe really sounded desperate and at the end of his rope. He was running out of options. I just had to help my friend. This really makes things even tougher for me. I have to find out what happened to the whole Emoji gang, and prom night is getting closer. I still don't have a date for it! This is really bad! How am I going to solve all of this?

ENTRY 6: EVERYONE VANISHES

"So have you heard about the entire Emoji gang disappearing?"

I asked Patty about the disappearances. I was able to get another free pass for prom preparations from Joe. I thought it was a good idea to excuse myself. After all, this way I could be hitting two birds with one stone. I could ask around about the disappearances and investigate, while also preparing for prom night which was fast approaching.

"I think everyone's heard about all that. Those disappearances of your classmates was pretty big news around campus, Noob. But there's more."

"Really? What's that?"

"There have been disappearances all over the school."

"Whoa!"

Now that was really big news! I thought that the disappearances were happening in our single class but now I realized that it was happening all over the school. I think this proved that Levi could not have been responsible for the disappearances. But it was still pretty possible that he had something to do with the Emoji gang disappearing. Other disappearances all over school, though? That was just crazy! This was really big and Joe would really want to hear about this. I had to tell him at the soonest time possible.

"I know. At the rate it's going, there won't be anyone around to have a prom night!"

"That's terrible! We have to do something!" I said.

"What can we do? We don't even have the faintest idea where to start."

Patty was getting desperate and I really couldn't blame her. I was also at a loss as for what to do.

"Come on. Let's go to Joe, my teacher. Maybe he'll know what to do."

"I heard about your teacher. They say he's a bit lazy to teach subjects but he's nice and smart. Okay."

We both ran to my classroom eager to tell Joe what Patty had revealed to me. Once we entered my classroom I got the shock of my life. Joe was there, but there was no one else in the room.

"Joe! What happened to everyone?" I asked.

"I hoped that you could shed some light on that. Everyone just didn't go to school today. I guess we all know what happened."

The three of us didn't even say anything. We all knew they had disappeared. This was really bad.

"Oh man. What are we going to do now? I just raced here to tell you about what Patty said."

"You have info?" Joe asked.

"Kinda. But pardon my manners. Joe, this is Patty, my friend at the prom committee.'"

"Hi Mr. Joe. I've heard good things about you."

"Thanks Patty. I wish we could have met under better circumstances. Well, what's the info you've got Noob?"

"These disappearances aren't just isolated to our class. It's been happening all over school." I said.

"That's great detective work Noob, but I already know it."

"You do?"

"Yeah. I did a little asking myself and I heard that the disappearances are happening all over school at a really rapid rate now. Lots of classes have been disappearing everywhere. When I went to class today, I realized that our class was the latest victim."

"This is just awful! There have probably been even more disappearances now while we were talking!" Patty said.

"This looks pretty bad. What'll we do now?"

"It does look bad, but maybe we can still solve the mystery." Joe said.

"How?"

"Before the whole class disappeared, I asked around and I heard that a certain dog-faced student was lurking around before the disappearances happened. We both know what this means Noob"

A Dog-faced student! My heart raced when Joe said those words. Could it be who I thought it was?

"Yeah. I think Frank is back and he's causing the disappearances!"

Joe completed my train of thought. I didn't want to believe it, but this looked like the most likely scenario. After all, this is so similar to Murder Mystery! Players disappearing one by one – it is definitely Frank's style. And of course, he would want to have revenge on Joe and me! This was terrifying. Knowing Frank, there is always something bigger behind his plans. If he is responsible for the mischief, I am scared to even think of what happened to the victims.

"Frank? Who's that?" Patty asked.

"You wouldn't want to know. Anyway,

I've got a plan but I'll need you and Patty to pull it off!"

Joe hastily explained his plan to us. It wasn't much, but it was all we had going for us now. It was now or never. Well, we'll be doing this in a few moments. Wish us luck!

ENTRY 7: MISSION X

Well, the plan was simple enough. Joe had learned from the janitor that the mystery dog-faced student had often frequented the auditorium. We thought this was probably the best place to catch him red-handed. Patty was a student so she would just simply hang out at the auditorium while me and Joe waited in a safe spot. Once Frank shows up, Patty will talk to him and hopefully this will lead us to some real answers. But I also felt bad for using Patty as our bait. I really grew to care for her these past few days! I also cannot believe that these students are in danger because of me and Frank's vendetta against me. I can't help but feel guilty...

We passed by several empty classrooms. This was really getting crazy. So many students had already disappeared and the school had turned as quiet as a graveyard. Patty walked ahead of us, while we followed from behind.

"Is this a good idea making Patty the bait for Frank?" I asked.

"You have any better ideas?" Joe countered.

"None, but I'm worried about her. You know how crazy Frank can be."

"I do, but I also don't see any other choice we have to get to the bottom of this."

I didn't answer Joe. He had a great point.

We finally made it to the auditorium. We hid behind the wall, and Patty entered. We could still see her as she went inside. We didn't have long to wait. Soon enough, a dog-faced student approached Patty. We were hidden behind the wall so we could make out his body, but we still couldn't make out who he really was. They talked for awhile, and he finally led Patty down a long hall.

"Quick! Follow them!"

I was really beginning to worry now. What will Frank do to her?!

We kept pace with the two of them, until they walked through the wall backstage.

"What?!" Joe exclaimed.

"We don't have time, Joe! Frank could be hurting Patty right now. Quick jump through the wall like they did!"

I got my cape out, and literally jumped through the wall, ending up on the floor in some space other than the auditorium. As I tried to get up, Joe landed on me and kept me down.

"What's happening?" Joe raised his voice,

slightly scared.

I looked around while getting up and saw Patty and Scrappy Randy. Soon I realized there were other students behind them. In fact, everyone was there, from Levi and EU to the Emoji gang who were now back to their old selves! But it was strange – they were just having fun bouncing around and socializing.

"What the hell is happening?" I exclaimed.

"What is going on here?" Joe asked.

I turned to face the mysterious student.

"Give us some answers now!"

"Don't hurt me!"

The mystery student turned and we immediately recognized him. It wasn't Frank.

"Scott! What are you doing here?"

It was Scott – the person we mistook for Frank back in Murder Mystery because of their similar appearance. It seemed like I just kept bumping into my old playmates wherever I went.

"Doing what you're all doing! Playing Roblox High School! I discovered this secret room backstage and it was just too cool to keep to myself. There are many secret room in Roblox High School – like the one in the lunch room. But the teachers knew about them while no one has been here before. So I decided to invite other students to join me and cut class here!

"This is nuts!" I said.

"Not really! It's actually a lot of fun!" EU said.

"And I've actually talked with the Big Gang, and I explained that the effects of my potion were only temporary. We had so much time to talk here and iron out our differences! We're all good friends now!" Levi said.

"Hey. I kinda like the Emoji gang better, and I think it's time we all stopped bullying." Stipples said.

I couldn't believe this. I never thought I would see the day that Levi would be friends with the entire Emoji gang! Well, that was definitely not a bad thing.

"Everybody get back to school! You're all in detention for a week!" Joe said.

Everyone went back up but booed and hissed at Joe. He wasn't popular with the students anymore but he was just doing his job.

"All's well that ends well! The missing students are all accounted for, and the prom can continue on schedule!" Patty said.

"Well, there is one last thing that hasn't been settled." I said.

"What's that?" she asked.

"Well, ever since I started playing, I've

been so busy that I wasn't able to get a date. With the prom coming up well, I still don't have a date and,"

I was really shy but I had to ask Patty out. She was a great girl and I really began to like her after all the adventures we had been through.

"Well, Patty, can you be my date for the prom?"

I was surprised at Patty's reaction. She jumped right at me and hugged me.

"I thought you would never ask Noob!"

So that's how it all ended. Everyone went back to class, or not really, because they all spent a week in detention. But at least they were all safe. Prom is in a couple of days and I am really happy that I am going with Patty.

But I won't lie, I am a bit concerned because Frank wasn't behind the disappearances. Don't get me wrong –

there is nothing in the world I wouldn't give to forget about that guy. Still, when I thought he was behind the "mischief," I knew where he was and what he was doing. Now that I've discovered that he had nothing to do with it, I have no idea where he is and what he is doing. I know he won't forget about what happened back in Murder Mystery. Now not only Marty, but Joe and I are also his enemies, and I know that he will stop at nothing to have his revenge on us.

Still, I managed to solve another mystery – not bad for a Noob like me! Actually, I've missed the excitement of uncovering hidden plots and saving lives. Perhaps I won't stay on one server after all, and will instead venture into the unknown to rediscover the high jazz of adventure...

-The End-

Thank you for reading this book! If you enjoyed my story, please leave a review on Amazon and sign up for future books at twomammons@gmail.com

Best wishes,

Robloxia Kid

Made in the USA
Middletown, DE
13 March 2017